This edition first published in Great Britain in 2016 by
ANDERSEN PRESS LIMITED
20 Vauxhall Bridge Road
London SW1V 2SA
www.andersenpress.co.uk

Reprinted 2017

British Library Cataloguing in
Publication Data available.

ISBN 978 1 78344 487 8

Printed and bound in Turkey by Omur Printing Co., Istanbul

The Little Book of Christmas Jokes

Illustrated by Nigel Baines

ANDERSEN PRESS

Santa Claus
Jokes

Why did Father Christmas start sneezing as he went down the chimney?

Because he had the flue.

What did Santa say when Mrs Claus asked about the weather?

'Looks like rain, dear.'

What did Father Christmas's wife call him when he became grammar-obsessed?

Santa Clause.

What goes, 'Oh! Oh! Oh!'?

Father Christmas walking backwards.

Why did Santa get a parking ticket?

He left his sleigh in a 'snow parking zone'.

4

Who looks after Father Christmas when he's ill?

The National Elf Service.

Father Christmas's sleigh broke down on Christmas Eve. He flagged down a passing car and asked,

'Can you help me fix my sleigh?'

'Sorry,' replied the driver, 'I'm not a mechanic, I'm a foot doctor.'

'Well then, can you give me a tow?'

6

What do you call a man who claps at Christmas?

Santapplause.

What do you get if you cross Father Christmas with a detective?

Santa Clues.

7

Why does Father Christmas have a garden?

Because he likes to hoe-hoe-hoe.

What do you call a smelly Santa?

Farter Christmas.

Reindeer Jokes

Did Rudolph go to school?

No, he was elf-taught.

What do reindeer say before telling a joke?

'Listen carefully, this one will sleigh you.'

Why did the reindeer wear sunglasses to the beach?

He didn't want to be recognised.

What do reindeer have that no other animals have?

Baby reindeer.

If a reindeer lost his tail, where would he go for a new one?

A re-tail shop.

Which reindeer has the worst manners?

Rude-olph.

How do you know if there's a reindeer in your fridge?

Look for hoof prints in the butter.

Why did Father Christmas call two of his reindeer 'Edward'?

Because two Eds are better than one, of course.

How can Santa's sleigh possibly fly through the air?

You would too if you were pulled by flying reindeer.

How do you get into Rudolph's house?

Ring the deer-bell.

Why do the reindeer love Father Christmas so much?

Because he fawns over them.

What's the difference between a reindeer and a biscuit?

You can't dunk a reindeer in your tea.

Elf Jokes

How would you describe a rich elf?

Welfy.

How long should an elf's legs be?

Just long enough to reach the ground.

Elfvis.

How many elves does it take to change a light bulb?

Ten. One to change the light bulb and nine to stand on each other's shoulders to reach it.

24

If there were
eleven elves, and
another one came along,
what would he be?

The twelf.

If athletes get athlete's foot, what do elves get?

Mistle-toes.

What do elves use to go from floor to floor?

An elfevator.

What do
elves write on
Christmas cards?

*Have a fairy
happy Christmas.*

**What is a
female elf called?**

A shelf.

**Why did Santa tell
off one of his elves?**

*Because he was goblin his
Christmas dinner.*

Why did the elf push his bed into the fireplace?

Because he wanted to sleep like a log.

Present
Jokes

'Can I have a wombat for Christmas?'

'What would you do with a wombat?'

'Play wom, of course.'

34

> **How do you make
> opening your Christmas
> presents last longer?**
>
> *Open them with boxing gloves on.*

Dear
Father Christmas,

Please may I have
a yellow door?

From
Sherlock Holmes.

Watson:
Why do you want
a yellow door,
Sherlock?

Sherlock:
Lemon-entry, my
dear Watson.

Who is a child's favourite king?

Stoc-King

What did the dog get for Christmas?

A mobile bone.

What do wizards use to wrap their presents?

Spell-o-tape.

Dear Father Christmas,

Could you please send me some crocodile shoes?

Father Christmas: 'Can't do that. He hasn't said what size shoes his crocodile wears.'

WHAT DID THE FARMER GET FOR CHRISTMAS?

A COW-CULATOR.

41

**Who delivers
presents to sharks
at Christmas?**

Santa Jaws.

Christmas Dinner Jokes

What beats his chest and swings from Christmas cake to Christmas cake?

Tarzipan.

Who is never hungry at Christmas?

The turkey – he's always stuffed.

'We had Grandma for
Christmas dinner this year.'

'Really? We had turkey.'

Why did the Christmas
cookie go to the doctor?

He was feeling crummy.

'Mum bought a huge turkey for Christmas dinner.'

'That must have cost a fortune!'

'Actually, she got it for a poultry amount.'

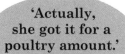

What do
vampires put
on their turkey
at Christmas?

Grave-y.

Last year's Christmas pudding was so awful I threw it in the sea.

That's probably why the ocean's full of currants.

How do you make Father Christmas stew?

You keep him waiting for half an hour.

'This turkey tastes like an old sofa!'

'Well, you asked for something with plenty of stuffing.'

Christmas Animal Jokes

What do fish do to celebrate Christmas?

They put reefs on the door.

What is white, lives
at the North Pole and
runs around naked?

A polar bare.

What do you
get when you cross
a bell with a skunk?

Jingle smells.

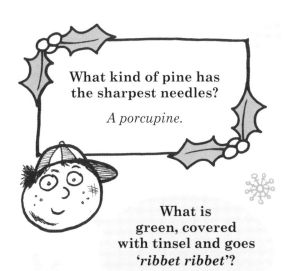

What kind of pine has the sharpest needles?

A porcupine.

What is green, covered with tinsel and goes 'ribbet ribbet'?

A mistle-toad.

57

What's white, furry and smells of mint?

A polo bear.

What do wild animals sing at Christmas time?

'Jungle bells, jungle bells, jungle all the way.'

Why do birds fly south for the winter?

Because it's too far to walk.

What do you call a cat on the beach at Christmas?

Sandy Claws.

What do angry mice send each other?

Cross-mouse cards.

What kind of bird can write?

A pen-guin.

Where do polar bears go to vote?

The North Poll.

What is six metres tall, has sharp teeth and says, 'Ho ho ho'?

Tyranno-santa Rex.

Christmas Complaints

'Doctor, doctor, Father Christmas gives us oranges every Christmas. Now I think I'm turning into one!'

'Have you tried playing squash?'

'Doctor, doctor, I keep thinking I'm a Christmas bell!'

'Just take these pills. If they don't work, give me a ring.'

'Nurse!
I want to operate.
Take this patient to
the theatre.'

'Oh good,
I love a nice
pantomime at
Christmas.'

Father Christmas: Doctor, doctor, I feel so unfit!

Doctor: *You need to go to an elf-farm.*

68

'Doctor, doctor, with all the excitement of Christmas, I can't sleep.'

'Try lying on the edge of your bed. You'll soon drop off.'

69

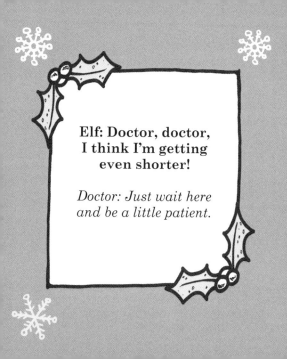

Festive
Knock Knock
Jokes

Knock knock
Who's there?
Mary.
Mary who?
Mary Christmas.

Knock knock
Who's there?
Avery.
Avery who?
Avery merry Christmas.

74

Knock knock

Who's there?

Carol singers!

*Carol singers? Do you know
what time of night it is?*

**No, but if you hum it,
we'll sing it.**

Knock knock

Who's there?

Rabbit.

Rabbit who?

Rabbit up neatly, it's a present.

Knock knock
Who's there?
Wendy.
Wendy who?

**Wendy red red
robin comes
bob bob
bobbin' along.**

Knock knock
Who's there?
Arthur.

Arthur who?
Arthur any mince pies left?

Knock knock

Who's there?

Wanda.

Wanda who?

Wanda know what you're getting for Christmas?

Christmas
Crackers

What did Adam say on the day before Christmas?

'It's Christmas, Eve.'

What do you have in December that you don't have in any other month?

The letter 'D'.

What do you call a letter
sent up the chimney
on Christmas Eve?

Black mail.

What says,
'Now you see me,
now you don't, now
you see me, now
you don't'?

*A snowman on
a zebra crossing.*

Who delivers
Christmas presents
to cats?

Santa Paws.

What does Father Christmas suffer from if he gets stuck in a chimney?

Santa claustrophobia.

What do snowmen eat for breakfast?

Frosties.

Why did the little girl change her mind about buying her grandmother a pack of hankies for Christmas?

Because she couldn't work out what size her nose was.

**What's a
good seasonal tip?**

*Never catch
snowflakes on your
tongue until all the birds
have flown south
for the winter.*

**What do you call an
old snowman?**

Water.

Christmas
Songs

What's a hairdresser's favourite Christmas carol?

'Oh Comb All Ye Faithful'.

What's a football supporter's favourite Christmas song?

'Yule Never Walk Alone'.

What's a dog's favourite
Christmas song?

'Deck the Howls'.

95

What's a rabbit's favourite Christmas carol?

'Lettuce with a Gladsome Mind'.

What's a talkative princess's favourite Christmas carol?

'Silent Knight'.

What do snowmen sing to Father Christmas?

'Freeze a Jolly Good Fellow'.

What's a farmer's favourite Christmas song?

'I'm Dreaming of a Wheat Christmas'.

Twinkle, twinkle
chocolate bar,
Santa drives a rusty car.
Press the starter,
Press the choke.
Off he goes in a
cloud of smoke!

Christmas Book Titles

The Art of Kissing
by Miss L. Toe

Winning at Charades
by Victor Ree

Guessing your Presents
by P. King

Bad Gifts
by M. T. Box

How to Receive a
Great Present
by B. Good

What to do After
Christmas Dinner
by Clare Inup

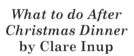

101 Cures for Indigestion
by Ivor Pain

The Twelfth Month
by Dee Sember

*Sledging for
Beginners*
by I. C. Bottom

Christmas Questions
by I. Dunnoe &
Noah Little

Surprise Presents!
by Omar Gosh

Make your Parents Buy you Everything
by Ruth Lesschild

*My Brother Hogs
all the Potatoes*
by Dick Tator

I'd Rather Have Fish for Christmas Dinner by Ann Chovie

Christmas Equations

Musical instrument +
Reindeer =

Organ Donner

**Christmas carol +
A dozen flowers =**

*The twelve daisies of
Christmas*

**Christmas carol +
Money =**

Jingle bills

**Really quiet +
Armed crusader =**

Silent knight

Reindeer + Cows =

Sleigh bulls

Snow + Frankenstein =
Snowball fright

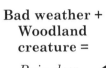

Bad weather + Woodland creature =

Rain deer

Spicy sauce + Christmas bow =

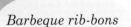

Barbeque rib-bons

Merry Christmas!

Collect them all!

The Funniest Animal Joke Book Ever

The Funniest Back to School Joke Book Ever

The Funniest Dinosaur Joke Book Ever

The Funniest Football Joke Book Ever

The Funniest Holiday Joke Book Ever

The Funniest Space Joke Book Ever

The Funniest Spooky Joke Book Ever